Lobo The Wolf
King Of Currumpaw

By Ernest Thompson Seton

Adapted by Storytellers Ink

Illustrated By Donna Ryan

Contents

Look for other Storytellers Ink
"Light Up The Mind Of A Child" Books:

Black Beauty
Beautiful Joe
Kitty the Raccoon
If a Seahorse Wore a Saddle
The Lost and Found Puppy
The Pacing Mustang
William's Story

Prologue

"This story is true.... The animals lived the lives I have depicted, and show the stamp of heroism and personality more strongly by far than it has been in the power of my pen to tell.

There is almost no deviation from the truth in Lobo. This wolf lived his wild romantic life from 1889 to 1894 in the Currumpaw region of New Mexico."

- Ernest Thompson Seton

Author Mark Steilen has added to Seton's story a depiction of the birth and early life of Lobo based on today's knowledge of wolves and their habits, in order to give the reader a more complete view of what it must have been like to be a grey wolf in the southwest United States in the 1890's.

- Storytellers Ink

Chapter I

A New Call

The largest wolf, his coat silver in the moonlight, stood poised at the steep edge of the mesa. His brother had not returned with him from the night's hunt. With narrowed eyes, concentrating, he lifted his head and stretched his neck, searching the breeze for messages carried in the night wind — he detected the soft scent of pinion trees, the bitter sage, the coolness rising from the river below. And there was something more. From a great distance, but clear and menacing, came the scent of wood fire, horse sweat, and finally, ever so faintly, man.

The leader howled a long, single note that faded into silence. When he tried again, his mate, lean and grey, joined him, harmonizing. She stood behind him near the entrance to the den where their three pups were wrestling.

The biggest of the pups, a grey and brown male, stopped playing and untangled himself. Sensing something important, he watched his mother carefully. His brother and sister followed his gaze and stared at their mother.

Lifting his head, he, too, tried his small voice, though he didn't understand yet what was happening, only that this was a new call, a sad song. The howls echoed, bouncing off the rocks of the mesa, but there was no reply from the river valley below.

When the silence returned, their father started back down the steep trail, retracing the steps he'd taken only a short while earlier when he'd come back alone. The grey wolf nosed each of her pups back into the den and followed after him.

One of the pups, the same who had been first to take up the howling, and to whom the other two already deferred, darted out of the opening, intending to join his parents. But when his mother heard his footsteps, she turned to him and gave a low growl, so he instantly retreated back into the den.

He lay down at the entrance, his head resting on his forepaws, watching and waiting.

The grandfather also stayed behind, lying down in the grass close enough to keep an eye on the entrance of the den, but far enough away so as not to give away its location. One adult wolf always remained at home to watch over the pups.

The den, with its long, narrow entrance hidden in the rocks, and its dark, cozy interior, had been all the pups had known for the first few weeks of their lives. Here they lived off their mother's milk, even before their eyes were open, snuggling up to her belly, scrambling and pushing for their meal, guided only by the scent and warmth of their mother.

The lessons that were necessary for their survival began here. The mother was always affectionate, nuzzling each of them, bathing them with her soft, warm tongue, and letting them crawl and nip and play all over her for hours at a time, but she was also stern in her discipline.

Once their eyes opened, each became very attracted to the light from the den opening. But the outside world was still too dangerous for them. Their plump little bodies could not yet move fast enough to evade foxes or hawks, who would make a quick meal of the pups if they were caught alone. Nor did they understand enough of the world to defend themselves.

This biggest pup had again been the first of the litter to dash towards the light of the den door, but his mother's discipline, a swift nip on his ear and a swat of her paw sent him rolling back into the dark and crashing into his brother and sister. It had been enough to teach him that he would not be allowed outside until his mother decided it was time.

By the time they were allowed to venture out into the sunlight and their strange new world, one of his brothers had already died. He had been small, and had lost in the competition for milk. When game was hard to find, and there was no meat for their parents, their mother's milk nearly dried up, leaving only enough for the strongest pups. Too weak to keep up, he hadn't lived through one of the times when they had to survive with little to eat.

It was here, in the safety of the den, that it had already become clear that

the biggest pup was, of the three who'd survived the first few weeks of life,

to be the one who took his father's place someday as the pack leader.

Somehow his nose led him more quickly to his mother's teat, his legs,

more powerful than his brother's or sister's, scrambled quickly over their

backs and heads for his feeding. His eyes found their way more surely in the

blackness of the den, and his curiosity led him first into each new adventure,

while his intelligence insured that he only needed to be taught a lesson once.

Later, when they were allowed to play outside the den, rolling, scrambling about in make-believe hunts, tackling each other and nipping at ears with their baby teeth, it was the biggest one who's balance, coordination and size turned the others upside down, toppling them, his mouth around their throats, but never in more than play.

They didn't know they were learning vital skills, like how to use one's weight to bring another down, when to hold on tight and when to let go, and how to anticipate being bitten, kicked, tripped or rolled — before it had a chance to happen.

It was all affectionate play. Each of the family members took time out

to romp with the pups. The games, hide and seek, tag, the wrestling, always ended with nose rubbing and kisses. But what was being learned would be applied in a world where mistakes, like not seeing or hearing or smelling keenly enough, could mean starvation or death.

As the mother began to push them from her milk, they were given their first taste of game. Returning from a kill, she would bring up some of her own meal for them, already partially digested. Thus they were introduced to the taste and scent of the different animals hunted by the pack. The rabbit and mouse, deer and antelope, were already familiar to the pups long before they ever saw them running by, or tracked a live scent on a trail or near a burrow.

When they became old enough to travel, the parents began to move them from one den to another. After a narrow miss when a bobcat found the den, and was frightened off by the grandfather only at the last minute, the pups understood the value of moving often to keep from being discovered. Too long in any one place could be very dangerous.

One particular night as the pair of wolves disappeared back down the trail, the biggest pup scooted forward in the den entrance. He was determined to stay awake to learn what was so important that his parents had to leave again so close to morning, when the night hunt should have ended. Convinced that his grandfather had fallen asleep, he started to sneak down the trail, but the old wolf rose and moved closer, making it clear that the pup had tested his limits enough for one night. The grandfather heaved a great sigh, and nestled in next to his grandson.

"Your uncle will not come back," the grandfather whispered. "The new men have killed him." The pup only waited, listening. His grandfather was no longer fast, nor as strong, and his sense of smell and eyesight faded more each day. But he stayed alive by his wits, making up for his body's growing weakness with his experience and cleverness.

"Everything that I was taught about how to hunt and how to survive, I taught your father. And your mother and father will teach you, too. For all of history, it has been that way, and it was enough. But it will not be enough much longer. The world is different now. The dangers are unseen, often impossible to smell. Death comes from far away. It does not face you. You will have to learn more than our history can teach."

As the first light pushed back the stars, the leader and his mate returned, but the pup's uncle was not with them. The pup was learning, yet not always understanding.

Chapter II

Learning To Hunt

Only a few months after his uncle had been killed, the big pup, who would be known as Lobo, and his siblings, were allowed to join the hunts. At first they could only watch and learn. They tried to keep up with the swift, strong adults by paying attention to the methods they used to find food even when the snows had driven the small animals underground and the large ones far away.

Lobo grew quickly – his puppy fat turning to muscle, his bones stretching, making him taller than any of the other wolves in the family.

His first success on his own as a hunter had been to track down a grouse that had been nesting in a hollowed log. He had waited patiently at the end of the log, crouched low to the ground, very still as if frozen for several hours, determined to match his patience to the grouses' need for food. And that evening, when the grouse, convinced the wolf had given up and gone away, stuck his head out of the log. Lobo snatched him up and carried him back to his family, holding his head high, happy to be helping for the first time.

His success as a hunter helped him gain size and strength until it was evident he would soon be larger than his own father. But always it was clear to him that, though he was strong, there was no substitute for the knowledge and experience his parents and grandfather had, and he carefully followed their instructions and did as he was told, knowing his life depended on it.

One evening, near the end of summer the pack prepared a favorite

strategy to hunt deer who made their beds deep in the thickets near a creek in one of the valleys. The younger wolves would start at one end of the valley, and chase the deer down and out of the trees, herding them along a narrow game trail that followed the creek. Deer were too quick for a single wolf to catch on the run, but at the other end of the valley, crouching low in the deep grass of a meadow, Lobo's father, mother and grandfather would hide and wait, springing on the deer as it passed them.

The groups split up, moving silently and stealthily into the trees. Lobo knew he'd reached the creek by the touch of the soft, cool moss under his feet. His brother would be in the brush to his left, his sister on his right. Having reached the creek, Lobo turned and followed it down the valley.

They moved soundlessly for some time when Lobo suddenly tensed. He detected the recent scent of a deer. But just as he paused, the deer shot out of their beds in the thicket ahead of him. One young buck with only stumps for antlers flashed away into the dark. A large doe followed him.

It was the last deer out of the thicket that Lobo decided to chase. He was an immense old buck with massive antlers, his sharp hooves still powerful enough to cave in the skull of an unlucky wolf, his horns able to pierce flesh – like swords. But the old buck moved with a limp, his right rear leg dragging slightly, possibly from a fight long ago. Even with the limp, the buck plunged well ahead of the wolves down the valley, his old body still strong.

Lobo ran hard, but not at full speed. It wasn't necessary for him to catch up to the buck, only to keep him near the small trail that ran the length of the valley. Patience was more important. He knew that fear and the sprint would tire the deer.

When he could see the stars peeking through the trees, Lobo's excitement grew. His parents would be just ahead, keeping low in the grass of the meadow, ready to surprise the fleeing deer.

The buck reached the clearing at full speed, his limp not slowing him down as much as Lobo had hoped it would.

The old deer dashed across the meadow and, with no sign of the wolves, vanished up into the cliffs. Puzzled, Lobo paused, not wanting to take his eyes off the buck that might be their only meal for many days. His brother and sister had appeared at a distance on his left and his right. They stopped too.

Then Lobo saw his mother and father. The buck had run right past them, but they looked as if they hadn't even looked up. The three young wolves trotted up the trail toward their parents. The grandfather lay on his side, not breathing. He was dead.

Lobo smelled sheep's blood and then saw the carcass on the other side of the trail near his grandfather's body. There was another smell, strange and

faint, barely discernible, mixed with the sheep's blood, a smell his grandfather's old nose had missed. Lobo began to understand it had something to
do with his grandfather being dead.

His mother and father stood stiff-legged, and then slowly they began
to back away from that part of the trail. With a whimper, Lobo's brother
approached his dead grandfather. Their mother growled, warning him not to
go any further, but he did.

The father leaped towards his son, but was too late. The heavy steel trap
concealed in the earth slammed against the bones of his brother's leg, and he
gave a howl of pain that echoed throughout the valley.

Confused and enraged, Lobo made a lunge at the vicious trap that held his brother, but Lobo's father shouldered him away, knocking him back to the other side of the game trail. As Lobo rolled, he heard the snap – snap – snap of the traps that he had set off and that had been waiting for him. His father had saved his life, for he had known that the sheep carcass was poisoned bait, and had correctly suspected other dangers.

Lobo's mother suddenly lifted her head. Another scent, one Lobo would never mistake again, had caught her attention. She turned back toward the trees, but in her first step, a crackling noise and a flash of light from the hillside knocked her down. Another crack, and another, each with a flash of light, sent tiny spits of dirt flying around the wolves' feet. Lobo's father sent them all running as fast as they could toward the trees.

The crackling noises followed them. Just inside the trees, Lobo's father turned back one last time, deciding whether or not to return for his mate, and in that pause, he, too, was hit by a bullet and killed.

In the flash of light, Lobo had seen the ghostly man's face, the rifle tucked against his cheek as he rode his horse, firing at them from the hillside above. Now the burning scent of sulphur scratched at Lobo's nose, merging with the dangerous scent of the man, and he and his sister moved back up the valley, out of reach of the gun, their family dead and dying, poisoned, trapped and shot.

This land where his family died that night was changing. New inhabitants were moving in. The rich land, which had evolved from earliest times into a vast sea of grasses that rippled and waved in the wind, was beckoning to them. As the Plains got closer to the Rocky Mountains, the grasslands began to break into rolling mesas.

Rain and snow draining off the hills created rivers and creeks that wove through the plush range. Currumpaw was one such creek in northeastern New Mexico, where the unaltered vast stretches of the Oklahoma Plains finally rumpled and started to rise. And as the land changed, stands of pinion and scrub pine began to appear.

For thousands of years, grazing animals – the buffalo, antelope, deer and elk – lived off the rich rangeland. And for just as long, predators – wolves, coyotes, mountain lions and Indians – fed off of these great herds, helping keep each species strong. For thousands of years, each depended on the other, in a natural balance of predator and prey.

The first humans in New Mexico were hunters like the wolves. They lived off the game they were able to kill with sharpened sticks and stones. They followed the vast herds, killing only what they needed. To them, the supply must have seemed endless.

These people lived in harmony with all the animals and plants in their world. The Navajo, Utes and Comanche tribes were hunters and gatherers,

people who lived as part of the system of predator and prey, of the natural order that had sustained both themselves as a species and the earth itself.

At the time of Lobo's birth, the Indians, who understood the value and importance of the environment and the animals and plants, had been forced onto reservations or killed in battles fought over the land. Many of the game animals had been killed for food, for clothing, or chased away to protect the businesses of ranching. And now only the new men and their herds of sheep and cattle were allowed in the area where he was born, the place named after the creek that ran out of the hills – Currumpaw.

But Lobo and the wolves had no way of understanding this new order.

The wolves only knew that they had always lived there.

And on this night, howling for the loss of his family, with a bitterness that came from deep inside him, Lobo prepared to fight back.

From that tragic night on he did fight. It was not a long time, measured in the life of one man, before he had become a legend. And Lobo, or the king, as the Mexicans called him, soon grew to be the gigantic leader of a pack of grey wolves that ranged over the Currumpaw Valley for years. All the shepherds and ranchers knew him well, and, wherever he appeared with his

trusty band, terror reigned among the cattle on his territorial homeland, and wrath and despair among their owners. Old Lobo was indeed a giant among wolves, and was cunning and strong in proportion to his size.

His voice at night was well-known and easily distinguished from that of any of his fellows. An ordinary wolf might howl half the night around the herdsman's camp without attracting more than a passing notice, but when the deep roar of the old king came booming down the canyon, the watcher bestirred himself and prepared to learn in the morning that fresh and serious inroads had been made among the herds.

Chapter III

Lobo's Band

Lobo's band was but a small one. Usually, when a wolf rises to the position and power that he had, he attracts a numerous following. It may be that he had as many as he desired, or perhaps his requirements of his band allowed only for the best.

Certain it is that Lobo had only five followers during the latter part of his reign. Each of these, however, was a wolf of renown, most of them were above the ordinary size, one in particular, the second in command, was a veritable giant, but even he was far below the leader in size and prowess. Several of the band, besides the two leaders, were especially noted.

One of these was a beautiful white wolf that the Mexicans called Blanca; this was supposed to be a female, possibly Lobo's mate. Another was a yellow wolf of remarkable swiftness, which, according to current stories had, on several occasions, captured an antelope for the pack.

It will be seen, then, that these wolves were thoroughly well-known to the cowboys and shepherds. They were frequently seen and often heard, and their lives were intimately associated with those of the cattlemen, who would so gladly have destroyed them.

There was not a stockman on the Currumpaw who would not readily have given the value for many steers for the scalp of any one of Lobo's band, but these wolves seemed to possess charmed lives, and defied all manner of devices to kill them. They scorned all hunters, derided all poisons, and continued, for at least five years, to exact their tribute from the Currumpaw ranchers as the band tried to drive from their land the alien ranchers.

The old idea that a wolf was constantly in a starving state, and therefore ready to eat anything, was as far as possible from the truth, for these wolves were sleek and well-conditioned, and were in fact most particular about what they ate.

Any animal that had died from natural causes, or that was diseased or tainted, they would not touch, and rejected anything that had been killed by the stockmen.

Many new devices for their extinction were tried each year, but still they lived and survived in spite of all the efforts of their foes.

A great price was set on Lobo's head, and so poison in a score of subtle forms was put out for him, but he never failed to detect and avoid it.

One thing only he feared – that was firearms, and he knew full well that all men in this region carried them. He never was known to attack or face a human being. Indeed, the set policy of his band was to take refuge in flight whenever, in the daytime, a man was detected, no matter at what distance.

Lobo's habit of permitting the pack to eat only that which they themselves had killed, was in numerous cases their salvation, and the keenness of his scent to detect the taint of human hands, or the poison itself, completed their immunity.

On one occasion, one of the cowboys heard the all too familiar rallying-cry of Lobo, and stealthily approaching, he found the Currumpaw pack in a hollow, where they had killed a cow.

The man now rode up shouting, the wolves as usual retired, and he, having a bottle of strychnine, quickly poisoned the carcass in three places, then went away, knowing they would return to feed, as they had killed the animal themselves. But the next morning, on going to look for his expected victims, he found that, although the wolves had eaten the heifer, they had carefully cut out and thrown aside all those parts that had been poisoned.

The dread of this great wolf spread among the ranchers, and each year a larger price was set on his head, until at last it reached $1,000, an unparalleled wolf-bounty, surely; many a good man has been hunted down for less.

Chapter IV

Wolfhounds

Tempted by the promised reward, a Texas ranger named Tannerey came one day galloping up the canyon of the Currumpaw. He had a superb outfit for wolf-hunting – the best of guns and horses, and a pack of enormous wolf-hounds. Far out on the plains of the Panhandle, he and his dogs had killed many a wolf, and now he never doubted that, within a few days, Old Lobo would be a prize.

They started off bravely on their hunt in the gray dawn of a summer morning, and soon the great dogs gave joyous tongue to say that they were already on the track of wolves.

Within two miles, the wolf band of Currumpaw came into view, and the chase grew fast and furious.

The part played by the wolf-hounds was to surround their quarry, holding them at bay till the hunter could ride up and shoot them. This was usually easy on the open plains of Texas; but here a new feature of the country came into play, showing how well Lobo had chosen his range. Here the rocky canyons of the Currumpaw and its tributaries intersect the prairies in every direction.

Lobo at once made for the nearest of these and by crossing it got rid of the horsemen. His band then scattered and thereby scattered the dogs,

and when the band reunited at a distant point not all the dogs appeared, and the wolves, no longer outnumbered, turned on their pursuers and killed or wounded them all. That night when Tannerey mustered his dogs, only six of them returned, and of these, two were badly wounded.

Tannery made two other attempts to capture the royal wolf, but neither of them was more successful than the first. And on the last occasion his best horse met its death by a fall; so he gave up the chase in disgust and went back to Texas, leaving Lobo more than ever the ruler of the region.

In the spring of 1893, a rancher named Joe Calone, who had made an unsuccessful attempt to capture Lobo, had a humiliating experience, which seems to show that the big wolf simply ignored his enemies, and had absolute confidence in himself. Calone's farm was on a small tributary of the Currumpaw, in a picturesque canyon, and among the rocks of this very canyon, within a thousand yards of the house, Lobo and his mate selected their den and raised their family that season.

There they lived all summer, and avoided all of Joe's poisons and traps, as they rested securely among the recesses of the cavernous cliffs, while Joe vainly racked his brain for some method of smoking them out, or of reaching them with dynamite. But they escaped entirely unscathed, and continued their hunting as before.

Chapter V

A Plan

This history, gathered so far from the cowboys, I found hard to believe until in the fall of 1893, I made the acquaintance of the wily marauder, and came to know him probably better than anyone else.

Some years before, I had been a wolf-hunter, but my occupation since then had been of another sort, keeping me at a desk and stool. I needed a change, and when a friend, who owned a ranch on the Currumpaw, asked me to come to New Mexico to see if I could be of any help dealing with this legendary pack, I accepted the invitation, and eager to meet the king, I was soon in Lobo's region among the mesas.

I spent some time just riding about the rough country and it soon became quite clear to me that it would be worse than useless to pursue the wolves with hounds and horses. It would have to be poison or traps. Since we had no traps large enough, I set to work with poison.

I need not enter into the details of a hundred devices that I employed to circumvent this charmed wolf; there was no combination that I did not use; there was no manner of bait that I did not try; but morning after morning, as I rode forth to learn the result, I found that all my efforts had been useless.

The king was too cunning for me. A single instance will show his wisdom. Acting on the hint of an old trapper, I melted some cheese together with the kidney fat of a freshly killed heifer, stewing it in a china dish, and cutting it with a bone knife to avoid the taint of metal.

When the mixture was cool, I cut it into lumps, and inserted a large dose of poison. During the whole process, I wore a pair of gloves steeped in the blood of the heifer, and even avoided breathing on the bait.

When all was ready, I put them in a raw-hide bag rubbed all over with blood, and rode forth, dragging the liver and kidneys and the beef at the end of a rope. With this I made a ten-mile circuit, dropping a bait at each quarter of a mile, and taking the utmost care, always, not to touch any with my hands.

Lobo generally came into this part of the range in the early part of each week. This was Monday, and that same evening as we were about to retire, I heard the deep bass howl that could only be his. On hearing it one of the boys briefly remarked, "There he is, we'll see."

The next morning I went forth, eager to know the result of our work. I soon came on the fresh trail of the wolves, with Lobo in the lead – his track was always easily distinguished. An ordinary wolf's forefoot is four-and-a-half inches long, that of a large wolf four-and-three-quarters inches, but Lobo's, as measured a number of times, was five-and-a-half inches from claw to heel. I afterward found that his other proportions were in scale, for he stood three feet high at the shoulder, and weighed one-hundred-and-fifty pounds.

His trail, therefore, though obscured by those of his followers, was never difficult to trace. The pack had soon found the track of my drag, and as usual followed it. I could see that Lobo had come to the first bait, sniffed about it, and finally had picked it up.

Then I could not conceal my delight. "I've got him at last," I exclaimed; "I shall find him stark within a mile," and I galloped on with eager eyes fixed on the great broad track in the dust. It led me to the second bait and that also was gone. How I exulted, "I surely have him now and perhaps several of his band."

But there was the broad paw-mark still on the drag; and though I stood in the stirrup and scanned the plain, I saw nothing that looked like a dead wolf. Again I followed, to find now that the third bait was gone, and the wolf king's

46

track led to the fourth. There we learned that he had not really taken the bait at all, but had merely carried them in his mouth. Then having piled the three on the fourth, he scattered filth over them to express his utter contempt for my devices. After this he left and went about his business with the pack he guarded so effectively.

This was only one of many similar experiences which convinced me that poison was never going to destroy this wolf.

So I awaited the arrival of the traps.

Chapter VI

The Traps

When the wolf traps arrived, two other men and I worked a whole week to get them properly set out. We spared no labor or pains; I adopted every device I could think of that might help to insure success.

The second day after the traps were set, I rode out to inspect them, and soon came upon Lobo's trail running from trap to trap. In the dust I could read the whole story of his doings that night. He had trotted along in the darkness, and although the traps were very carefully concealed, he had instantly detected the first one. Stopping the onward marching of the pack, he had cautiously scratched around it until he had disclosed the trap, the chain, and the log, then left them wholly exposed to view with the trap still unsprung, and passing on he treated over a dozen traps in the same fashion.

Very soon I noticed that he stopped and turned aside as soon as he detected suspicious signs on the trail and a new plan to outwit him at once suggested itself. I set the traps in the form of an H; that is, with a row of traps on each side of the trail, and one on the trail for the cross-bar of the H.

Before long, I had an opportunity to count another failure. Lobo came trotting along the trail, and was fairly between the parallel lines before he detected the single trap in the trail, but he stopped in time, and why or how he knew enough I cannot tell. The angel of the wild things must have been with him, because without turning an inch to the right or left, he slowly and cautiously backed on his own tracks, putting each paw exactly in its old track until he was off the dangerous ground. Then returning at one side he scratched clods and stones with his hind feet till he had sprung every trap.

This he did on many other occasions, and although I varied my methods and redoubled my precautions, he was never deceived. His awareness seemed never at fault, and it looked like he would pursue his career into old age.

Chapter VII

A Trusted Alliance

Once or twice, I had found indications that everything was not quite right in the Currumpaw pack. There were signs of irregularity, I thought. For instance there was clearly the trail of a smaller wolf running ahead of the leader, at times, and this I could not understand until a cowboy made a remark which explained the matter.

"I saw them today," he said, "and the wild one that breaks away is Blanca." Then the truth dawned upon me, and I added, "Now, we know that Blanca is a female, because were another male to act as leader, Lobo would attack instantly and it would be a fight to the end."

This suggested a new plan. I killed a heifer, and set one or two rather obvious traps about the carcass. Then cutting off the head, which is considered quite beneath the notice of a wolf, I set it a little apart, and around it placed two powerful steel traps properly deodorized and concealed with the utmost care. During the operations I kept my hands, boots, and implements smeared with fresh blood, and afterward sprinkled the ground with the same, as though it had flowed from the head; and when the traps were buried in the dust I brushed the place over with the skin and paw prints of a coyote. The head was so placed that there was a narrow passage between it and some tussocks, and in this passage I buried two of my best traps, fastening them to the head itself.

Wolves have a habit of approaching every carcass they get wind of, in order to examine it, even when they have no intention of eating it, and I hoped that this habit would bring the Currumpaw pack within reach of my latest strategy. I did not doubt that Lobo would detect my handiwork about the meat, and prevent the pack from approaching it, but I did build some hopes on the head, for it looked as though it had been thrown aside as useless.

Next morning, I sallied forth to inspect the traps, and there, oh, joy! were the tracks of the pack, and the place where the beef-head and its traps had been was empty. A hasty study of the trail showed that Lobo had kept the pack from approaching the meat, but one, a small wolf, had evidently gone on to examine the head as it lay apart and had walked right into one of the traps.

We set out on the trail, and within a mile discovered that the hapless wolf was Blanca. Away she went, however, at a gallop, and although encumbered by the beef-head, which weighed fifty pounds, she speedily out-distanced my

companion who was on foot.

But we overtook her when she reached the rocks, for the horns of the cow's head became caught and held her fast. She was the handsomest wolf I had ever seen. Her coat was in perfect condition and nearly pure white.

She turned to fight, and raising her voice in the rallying cry of her race, sent a long howl rolling over the canyon. From far away upon the mesa came a deep response, the cry of the king. That was her last call, for now we had closed in on her, and all her energy and breath were devoted to combat.

Then followed the inevitable tragedy, the idea of which I shrank from afterward more than at the time. A lasso was thrown over her neck and our horses pulled until her eyes glazed, her limbs stiffened, and she fell limp. Then we rode away, carrying the wolf, the first death-blow we had been able to inflict on the Currumpaw pack.

At intervals during the tragedy, and afterward as we rode homeward, we heard the roar of Lobo as he wandered about on the distant mesas, where he seemed to be searching for Blanca. He had never really deserted her, but knowing that he could not save her, his deep-rooted dread for firearms had been too much for him when he saw us approaching. All that day we heard him wailing as he roamed in his quest, and I remarked at length to one of the boys, "Now, indeed, I truly know that Blanca was his mate."

As evening fell he seemed to be coming toward the home canyon, for his voice sounded continually nearer. There was an unmistakable note of sorrow in it now. It was no longer the loud, defiant howl, but a long, plaintive wail; "Blanca! Blanca!" he seemed to call.

And as night came down I noticed that he was not far from the place where we had overtaken her. At length he seemed to find the trail, and when he came to the spot where we had killed her, his heart-broken wailing was heart-wrenching to hear. It was sadder than I could possibly have believed. Even the stolid cowboys noticed it, and said they had "never heard a wolf carry on like that before." He seemed to know exactly what had taken place, for her blood had stained the place of her death.

Then he took up the trail of the horses and followed it to the ranch-house. Whether in hopes of finding her there, or in quest of revenge, I know not, but the latter was what he found, for he surprised our unfortunate watch-dog outside and tore him to little bits within fifty yards of the door.

I believed that he would continue in the neighborhood until he found her body at least, so I concentrated all my energies on this one enterprise of catching him before he left the region, and while yet in his reckless mood. Then I realized what a mistake I had made in killing Blanca, for by using her as a decoy I might have secured him the next night.

I gathered in all the traps I could command, one-hundred-and-thirty strong steel wolf-traps, and set them in fours in every trail that led into the canyon. Each trap was separately fastened to a log, and each log was separately buried.

When the traps were concealed I trailed the body of poor Blanca over each place, and made of it a drag that circled all about the ranch. Every precaution known to me I used, and retired at a late hour to await the result.

Once during the night I thought I heard Lobo, but was not sure of it. Next day I rode around, but by dark had nothing to report. At supper one of the cowboys said, "There was a great row among the cattle in the north canyon earlier, maybe there is something in the traps there."

It was afternoon of the next day before I got to the place referred to, and as I drew near, a grizzly form arose from the ground, vainly endeavoring to escape. There revealed before me stood Lobo, King of the Currumpaw, firmly held in the traps. Poor old hero, he had never ceased to search for his darling, and when he found the trail her body had made he followed it recklessly, and soon fell into the snare prepared for him. There he lay in the iron grasp of all four traps, perfectly helpless, and all around him were numerous tracks showing how the cattle had gathered about him to insult the fallen king, without daring to approach within his reach.

When I went near him, he rose up with bristling mane and raised his voice, and for the last time made the canyon reverberate with his deep bass roar, a call for help, the muster call of his band. But there was none to answer him, and, left alone in his extremity, he whirled about with all his strength and made a desperate effort to get at me.

Each trap was a dead drag of over three hundred pounds, and in their relentless fourfold grasp, with great steel jaws on every foot, and the heavy logs and chains all entangled together, he was absolutely powerless. His huge ivory tusks ground on those cruel chains, and when I ventured to touch him with my rifle-barrel, he left grooves on it which are there to this day. His eyes glared green with hate and fury, and his jaws snapped with a hollow 'chop,' as he vainly endeavored to reach me and my trembling horse. But he was worn out with hunger and struggling and loss of blood, and he soon sank exhausted to the ground.

Something like regret came over me, as I prepared to deal out to him that which others had suffered at his hands.

"Grand old outlaw, hero of a thousand raids, in a few minutes you will be but a great memory. It cannot be otherwise." Then I swung my lasso and sent it whistling over his head. But not so fast; he was yet far from being subdued, and, before the supple coils had fallen on his neck he seized the noose and, with one fierce chop, cut through its hard thick strands, and dropped it in two pieces at his feet.

Of course I had my rifle as a last resource, but I did not wish to spoil his valuable royal hide, so I galloped back to camp and returned with a cowboy and a fresh lasso. We threw to our victim a stick of wood which he seized in his teeth, and before he could relinquish it our lassos whistled through the air and tightened on his neck.

Yet before the light had died from his fierce eyes, I cried, "Wait, we will not kill him; let us take him alive to the camp." He was so completely power-less now that he made no further resistance, and uttered no sound, but looked calmly at us and seemed to say, "Well, you have got me at last." And from that time on, he took no more notice of us.

We tied his feet securely, but he never groaned, nor growled, nor turned his head. Then with our united strength we were just able to put him on my horse. His breath came evenly as though sleeping, and his eyes were bright and clear again, but did not rest on us. Afar on the great rolling mesas they were fixed; his passing kingdom, where his famous band was now scattered. And he gazed out over it till the pony descended the pathway into the canyon, and the rocks cut off his view.

By travelling slowly we reached the ranch in safety, and after securing him with a collar and a strong chain, we staked him out in the pasture and removed the cords.

Then for the first time I could examine him closely and prove how vulgar the rumors were about him. He had *not* a collar of gold, nor was there on his shoulders an inverted cross to denote that he had leagued himself with Satan.

But I did find on one haunch a great scar, that tradition says was the fang-mark of Juno, the leader of Tannerey's wolf-hounds – a mark which she gave him the moment before he stretched her lifeless on the sands of the canyon.

I set meat and water beside him, but he paid no heed. He lay calmly on his breast, and gazed with those steadfast yellow eyes away past me down through the gateway of the canyon, over the open plains – his plains – nor moved a muscle when I touched him. When the sun went down he was still gazing fixedly across the prairie. I expected he would call up his band when night came, and prepared for them, but he had called once in his extremity, and he would never call again.

A lion shorn of his strength, and eagle robbed of his freedom, or a dove bereft of his mate, all die, it is said, of a broken heart; and who will argue that this great wolf could bear the three-fold brunt, heart-whole? This only I know, that when the morning dawned, he was lying there still in his position of calm repose, but his spirit was gone.

I took the chain from his neck, a cowboy helped me to carry him to the shed where lay the remains of Blanca, and as we laid him beside her, the cattle-man exclaimed: "There, you *would* come to her, now you are together again."